sea country

We dedicate this book to our children's children

P.C. & L.K.

Leading Publisher of Aboriginal and Torres Strait Islander Storytellers.

Changing the World, One Story at a Time.

First published 2021, reprinted 2021, 2023 and 2025
Magabala Books Aboriginal Corporation
1 Bagot Street, Broome, Western Australia

Website: www.magabala.com Email: sales@magabala.com

Magabala Books is assisted by the Australian Government through Creative Australia, its principal arts investment and advisory body. The State of Western Australia has made an investment in this project through the Department of Local Government, Sport and Cultural Industries.

Reproduction photography by Splitting Image

Printed and bound in China by Everbest Printing Company Ltd

The illustrations in this book are mixed media, comprising graphite pencil, watercolours, paper collage and woodblock print.

Portrait page 10: Mannalargenna, circa 1775–1835: by Thomas Bock, circa 1831–1835
Portrait page 11: Granny Nancy Mansell, granddaughter of Mannalargenna: Photographer unknown

ISBN 978-1-925936-03-2 Print
ISBN 978-1-922613-06-6 ePUB

A catalogue record for this book is available from the National Library of Australia

Packaged by Ballantyne Rawlins in collaboration with Magabala Books.

FSC® is a non-profit international organisation established to promote the responsible management of the world's forests.

sea country

AUNTY PATSY CAMERON & LISA KENNEDY

My people are
proud, strong people.

We are the descendants
of Mannalargenna
of the Pairrebeenne /
Trawlwoolway clan.

We grew up on Flinders Island
in eastern Bass Strait.

The bush and the beach
were our playground.

There was freedom there.
Freedom to practise our culture.
To know who we were
and where we came from.

Granny Nancy Mansell,
granddaughter of
Mannalargenna

shell collecting on the beach

Aunties all around.

Collecting shells,

stringing them into necklaces.

Uncles all around.

Rice shells, toothies, black crows, penguins, mairreeners, oat shells, gull shells.

black crows
toothies
penguins
rice shells
looking for mairreeners
growing on seaweed when
the tide turns
gull
shells
oat shells

garfish
flounder
mutton
fish

Fishing with their nets,
in their wooden dinghies
with long oars.

We children would look for shellfish
to cook and eat.

We were free to hear Country speaking to us —
to watch for signs from Country.

A ring around the moon told us bad weather was coming.

Grandfather Silas showed us what Country was saying.
When the clouds came down over Mount Munro,
the rains would come and the wind would blow
from the south-east.

When the
black cockatoos
came down from the mountains,
we knew it would rain, and the winds
would blow from the north-west.

When the boobyallah flowers came,
it was time to look up.
This is when the mutton birds would come
in a great wave at dusk.
Circling overhead for hours,
turning the sky black.
They had travelled thousands of kilometres
and would land within a few metres
of their own nests from the years before.

YOLLA
Cape Barren geese
mutton birds lay just one egg per season in their burrow
We are prepared for the seasonal return of the Mutton birds with the help of Uncle Silas Mansell and his knowledge ♀
1948 This bird is very young maybe 2 yrs old and is now nesting in burrow ♀
1949 ♀ the female seems exhausted and dropped her egg outside the nest.
1950 ♀ They have returned from feeding on Krill in Antarctic waters.
Fisher Island Rookery has about 150 pairs of breeding Mutton birds
An index of cards for each ringed bird
Field Notes ♀
12591
1948 Nov; Burrow 297; bred; mated with 12310
1949 " " 297; mate unknown
1950 " " 297; mated with 12310
1951 " 297; " " 12310
1952 " 297; " " 12310
1953 " 297; " " 12461
"Patricia" the Mutton bird returns every year to lay her egg. She is named after me! Patricia
banded
webbed feet for swimming not walking.
"We put Seaberry Saltbush juice on our lips to make them red!" Patsy and Betty
Our lipstick bush.
Uncle Silas and I help the scientist Vincent Serventy who has come from mainland Melbourne, Australia, to study the habits of the birds. patsy.

wild cherries

wild currants

Summer is the season
for ripening.
Wild cherries,
wild currants,
tatas,
canygong.
Canygong fruits
taste like
salty strawberries.

tatas

canygong

We did not know where
the mutton birds had been
for so long.

We imagined them in the sea,
diving to catch the krill they eat,
talking with the whales.

The old people called
the mutton birds yolla.

We called them
moon birds,
as we imagined
them flying
to the moon
and back.

When the mutton birds would leave the island,
it was the time for paper nautilus shells.
The whole family walked for hours along the beach,
gathering the nautilus shells the sea had brought to us.

The shells smelled like the deepest ocean.
The old people called this shell wietenah.

These are some of the the ways
that Sea Country showed us
another year had passed.

“In the early 1800s, cotton thread and sewing needles were introduced to our people’s tool kits.

The women made necklaces using a range of small shells and stringing them into beautiful patterns.

When I was young, I watched my mum stringing shells the way her old aunties had taught her. She told me that the aunties from

Cape Barren Island showed her where to gather toothies and rice shells on the island beaches. They showed her how to clean the shells and string them into patterns. Mum always used mairreener shells in her patterns like this exquisite green necklace.

Now I make my own strings of shells just as my mum taught me to make. ”

AUNTY PATSY CAMERON, 2021

PATSY CAMERON grew up on Flinders Island and can trace her Tasmanian Aboriginal heritage through her mother's line to four ancestral grandmothers; Pleenpereener, Wyerlooberer, Teekoolterme and Pollerelbrener. At the head of her family is Teekoolterme's father, the revered Pairrebeene/Trawlwoolway clan leader, formidable warrior and seer, Mannalargenna.

Patsy has a Bachelor of Arts degree, a Master of Arts in Tasmanian Aboriginal History and an Honorary Doctor of Letters from the University of Tasmania. Her book *Grease and Ochre* was published in 2011.

Patsy was inducted onto the Tasmanian Women's Honour roll in 2006 and was invested with an Officer of the Order of Australia (AO) in 2017 for distinguished service to Indigenous communities in Tasmania.

LISA KENNEDY is descended from Woretemoeteryenna, daughter of Mannalargenna of the Pairrebeene/ Trawlwoolway clan.

Lisa began her artistic working life in community Victoria, mentored by experienced artists and Elders as well as studying visual art at the Victorian College of the Arts and Monash University, Gippsland.

Lisa has illustrated many award-winning books for young people, including *Welcome to Country* and *Wilam*, published by Black Dog Books. Her most recent book is *Respect* by Aunty Fay Muir and Sue Lawson, published by Magabala Books.

Lisa feels creatively blessed to have worked alongside Aunty Patsy Cameron on *sea country*.